THE WARRIOR'S ROAD

TARGRO
THE ARCTIC
MENACE

With special thanks to Gillian Philip

For Mosstowie Primary School

www.beastquest.co.uk

ORCHARD BOOKS
338 Euston Road, London NW1 3BH
Orchard Books Australia
Level 17/207 Kent St, Sydney, NSW 2000

A Paperback Original
First published in Great Britain in 2013

Beast Quest is a registered trademark of Beast Quest Limited
Series created by Beast Quest Limited, London

Text © Beast Quest Limited 2013
Inside illustrations by Pulsar Estudio (Beehive Illustration)
Cover illustration by Steve Sims © Orchard Books 2013

A CIP catalogue record for this book is available from
the British Library.

ISBN 978 1 40832 403 5

1 3 5 7 9 10 8 6 4 2

Printed in Great Britain by CPI Group (UK) Ltd, Croydon, CR0 4YY

The paper and board used in this paperback are natural recyclable
products made from wood grown in sustainable forests. The
manufacturing processes conform to the environmental regulations of
the country of origin.

Orchard Books is a division of Hachette Children's Books,
an Hachette UK company

www.hachette.co.uk

TARGRO
THE ARCTIC
MENACE

BY ADAM BLADE

ORCHARD

ICY
MOUNTAIN
REGION

ERRINEL

The Warrior's Road

COSHTIN PROVINCE

PYRUS

EAST CITY

MARBLE CASTLE

Greetings, whoever reads this.

I am Tanner, Avantia's first Master of the Beasts. I fear I have little time left. My life slips away, and I write these few words as a testament for whoever may come across my remains. I have reached the end of my final journey. But a new warrior's journey is just beginning...

With the death of a Master, a new hero must take on the responsibility of guarding the kingdom of Avantia. Avantia needs a true warrior to wear the Golden Armour. He or she must walk the Warrior's Road – a test of valour and strength. I have succeeded, but it has cost me my life. I only hope those who follow survive.

May fortune be with you,

Tanner

PROLOGUE

A cold breeze ruffled the owl's snow-white feathers as he tightened his talons on his keeper's shoulder, and scoured the landscape for prey.

"Hunting will be good now, Moray," said Luke, with a gentle tug on his tethering rope. "The skies have cleared, and creatures will be hungry after the storm."

Moray's gaze caught a tiny movement in the snow. A mouse skittered, and as Moray stretched his great wings, he felt Luke slip the cord from his leg. The snow-owl launched himself silently into the air.

The tiny creature didn't even see him coming. On noiseless wings, Moray swept down and snatched it into his talons, killing it instantly. With a screech of triumph he landed on the snow, folding his wings as he gulped the mouse down.

"Well caught, Moray!" cried Luke.

His hunger satisfied, Moray soared skywards again. Now he would hunt for Luke, too; he had worked with the human since he was a fledgling, and they were a good team. In return for his hunting skills, Luke gave him a warm place to shelter in these frozen mountains.

Moray blinked his eyes as a shadow appeared on the horizon. This animal was too big to be prey. Rising on the breeze, Moray soared towards it. What creature would dare invade his territory?

As he swooped closer, Moray gave a scream of shock. Losing his balance on the air currents, he began to tumble.

It was a fox – but not an ordinary one. Covered with glowing purple fur, its great clawed feet drove huge holes into the snow where it prowled. It came closer and closer, until it was directly beneath Moray. The creature was gigantic! Before Moray could stop himself, he'd let out a cry of alarm.

Immediately, the fox threw back its head. It gave a chilling scream and reared up on its hind legs. Moray beat his wings frantically and rose up – but not fast enough to avoid the slash of claws that were like giant shards of ice.

Moray shrieked at the sharp sting of pain. White tail feathers floated down through the icy air, splashed with blood. The owl felt his heartbeat skip, then he began to fall.

I'm injured! Moray wanted to fly far away from the Beast – but with his tail feathers damaged, he was hurtling towards the ground. Catching the wind at the last moment, Moray managed a clumsy swerve beneath the giant fox's belly. But the huge fox threw himself into a roll, sending plumes of snow flying as it crashed on its back on top of the owl. Huge, unnatural spikes on the creature's back pierced his wings, trapping him in the snow. Then the Beast sprang to its feet and thundered across the snow, Moray pinioned helplessly to its back.

Blood filled the owl's throat; he couldn't even screech. He heard Luke's cries of horror as the creature thundered towards him. Moray tried to get loose, but the fox's spikes pierced his flesh. *I'm not going to die. Not like this...*

With a last almighty wrench, Moray tore himself free of the giant fox, blood spattering into the snow. He could not even look back to see what had become of Luke – all he could hear were the terrified screams of his master, fading behind him. He could only fly wildly towards a pile of rocks, searching for a place to hide.

Luke was his best friend, yet there was nothing Moray could do to help him. Fear would not even let him look back, to see what had become of the man who had raised him from a tiny owlet. His dear master, his honour and his pride – would they ever see each other again?

CHAPTER ONE

THE FROZEN LAND

A blast of wind hurled snow into Tom's eyes. He flung up an arm to protect his face as he jumped down from the portal that had brought them from Errinel. The hole in the air shimmered, hovering just above the ground.

"The Warrior's Road!" gasped Elenna. She leaped down after him, her faithful wolf Silver right behind

her. "It's brought us to another land!"

Tom wiped snowflakes from his eyes and gazed at the hostile surroundings. "A land we're not prepared for," he said.

He could see that ice crystals were already forming in Elenna's hair. This snow-covered kingdom was nowhere near Errinel, Tom's home village, where they'd just defeated Skurik the Forest Demon. The blizzard howled like a fiend, blinding them and whipping ice against their skin. Within moments they were chilled to their bones.

"This is a dangerous place even without Beasts," Tom said grimly. "The Judge wants us to freeze to death before we even get a chance to complete our Quest!"

The evil sorcerer had stripped Tom of his status as Master of the Beasts. The Judge had set him a challenge to walk the deadly path once walked by Tanner, the very first Master. Tom had had no choice but to accept the Judge's challenge, even though it had been hundreds of years since anyone had survived the Road... If he didn't, he'd never win back his right to be Master of the Beasts and the whole of Avantia would be vulnerable.

"The Judge won't defeat us, Tom," Elenna said, squinting into the storm. "You will be Master of the Beasts again! No one else can protect Avantia."

Tom glanced around, but couldn't see anything in the whirling blizzard – not even the glowing red cobbles of the Road. "I can't see the Warrior's Road," he said. He was the only one the Road appeared to. "But we won't survive this weather unless we find shelter. We might have to go on, anyway, and just hope we're headed in the right direction."

His fingers numb, he pulled out his bloodstained map, but a wild gust of wind almost snatched it from his fingers. Clutching it, he tucked it frantically back into his tunic. *I can't lose the map!*

Tom took a few awkward steps. His leggings were quickly soaked through, and before long he fell forward, his arms sinking into the snow at the foot of a cliff. There was no way out of this storm. They'd end up buried in snow! *That's it,* Tom suddenly thought. *That's how we survive.*

"I've got it!" he shouted to Elenna. "We have to bury ourselves in the snow. It's the only way!"

Elenna kneeled at his side. "Are you sure, Tom?" she asked. "We might freeze!"

"As long as we stay huddled together," said Tom, "we'll be warm enough. Trust me."

Together they began to shovel out
a shallow pit with their bare hands.
Silver joined in, his paws throwing
aside huge clods of wet snow. *Thank
goodness we have Silver to help.*

Elenna's lips were turning blue

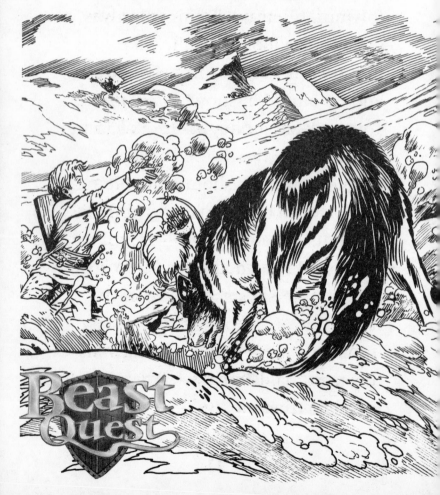

in the icy blast. If they weren't
fast enough, Tom knew, both his
fingertips and her lips would begin to
turn black, as frostbite sank its cruel
teeth into them.

We don't have much time...

"Quick, Elenna." Tom's voice was
hoarse. "It's big enough to take
the three of us. We can't wait any
longer!"

Elenna clambered down, and Tom
lay alongside her in the shallow
trough, gritting his teeth as he felt
the first shock of cold along his body.
Straightaway, though, Silver jumped
down and stretched himself out
between them. The warmth of the
wolf's powerful body began to seep
into Tom, and when he plunged his
fingers into Silver's thick fur, he could
feel them tingling. Before long, the

numb stiffness turned into stinging pain, but at least Tom's hands were thawed enough for him to tug the map from his tunic and roll it into a cylinder.

"This will keep an air hole open," he told Elenna. She was clinging onto Silver, her face buried in his fur.

The snow was falling more and more thickly, and they were soon covered in a thin layer. Dimly Tom could see light glowing through the icy coating. It was strangely quiet, the raging of the blizzard muffled. Tom could hear Silver's deep rumbling breath, and the warmth of his furred body was comforting.

"I've never been so glad to have Silver with us on a Quest," he murmured to Elenna.

"I know." Elenna rested her

face against the wolf's neck. In the dimness, Tom could see that her eyelids were drooping with exhaustion. Tom too felt himself growing steadily drowsier with the rise and fall of the wolf's ribcage.

No! One of us needs to stay awake! he thought, fighting the urge to give in. Yet the exhaustion of the struggle had drained his strength. *Surely I could close my eyes for a second...just for a second...*

But even as Tom tried to force his eyes back open, he felt sleep crash over him like a wave.

CHAPTER TWO

STRANGERS IN THE SNOW

A sharp pain shot through Tom's foot, and he woke with a cry of shock.

As he staggered to his feet, crusted snow fell away from his body. All around was blinding whiteness, and morning sunlight glittered off the landscape.

They had survived the bitter night after all! Their shallow snow-den had worked, protecting them from the worst of the blizzard. Tom stamped his foot to ease the cramp in his leg, feeling a surge of relief as he watched Elenna clamber groggily from the hole. Silver scratched his ear with a hind paw and shook snow from his fur.

A shout of fear broke the eerie silence. "Beasts! Deadly Beasts!"

Turning on his heel, Tom clutched the hilt of his sword. In the near distance, a group of people peered from behind a rock, their eyes wide with fear and anger. The man who had shouted pointed at Tom and Elenna, and one woman snatched a curious little boy back to her side.

"Monsters!" the woman cried. "Who are they?"

"No!" Tom seized Elenna's arm and helped her to her feet as Silver yelped encouragingly. "We're not Beasts."

Releasing his sword, Tom held out his hands in a peaceful gesture. *These people might be able to help us*, he thought. *If we can earn their trust.*

The strangers were emerging from behind their rock now, watching the three travellers carefully.

"You're only a boy!" exclaimed the

woman in surprise.

"A boy with a sword and a shield," muttered a man.

Tom gasped as the people approached. Despite the freezing temperatures, the women wore thin linen dresses and the men light tunics. Strangest of all, they weren't even shivering in the icy blasts.

"They're barefoot!" Elenna whispered.

His friend was right. One of the men strode forward, his bare feet sinking into the snow.

"Who are you?" he asked Tom.

"And what are you doing here?" said one of the women, with a hostile glance at Silver.

Tom placed a hand on Silver's head. "We're...travellers. Lost ones, I'm afraid." Tom gave them a rueful smile.

There wasn't any point telling them about the Warrior's Road or about his Quest. "Perhaps, if you know this country, you can help us?"

"And can you tell us how you survive the cold?" added Elenna, smiling. "Those clothes are so thin!"

A young girl tilted her head and frowned. "Never mind asking us questions. What were you two doing buried in the snow? That's the Fox-Beast's trick!"

"Aye," growled another man. "The Beast that haunts these mountains."

Tom shared a glance with Elenna. Were they close to a Beast? He wanted to ask more, but it was clear they'd have to explain themselves first.

"We were b-b-b-buried..." His teeth chattered so he could barely speak!

Another woman shouldered her way

to the front of the little group. "How can you ask them questions now?" she scolded her companions. "Can't you see they're freezing? These wanderers are no threat to us. Has the Fox-Beast made all of you forget our traditions?"

The others glanced at one another, a little shamefaced. "I'm sorry, Rana," muttered a tall bearded man. He glanced back at Tom. "We should offer you hospitality, not suspicion."

"That's better," said the woman called Rana. "Our fear of the Fox-Beast shouldn't make us terrified of every strange face."

"Thank you." Grateful for Rana's intervention, Tom returned her friendly smile. She had an air of calm authority, and her friends seemed quick to defer to her. *Thank goodness she's here*, Tom thought. *The others might have left us to freeze to death!*

"Maya!" The woman clapped her hands, turning to the girl. "Fetch cloaks for these weary travellers!"

The girl scampered back to her friends, her feet light on the snow. In moments she returned, bearing fine linen cloaks in her thin arms, and handed them shyly to Tom.

His teeth still chattering, Tom smiled his thanks. He gave Elenna a doubtful look. The cloaks Maya had brought looked as thin and insubstantial as the linen dress the child was wearing. *These won't be enough to guard us against the snow and ice!*

"Put them on," Rana commanded, but there was kindness in her voice as she draped the cloaks over their shoulders. "Our people travel across the cold mountains all the time to

trade and buy supplies at the coast.
I promise you, these are all the
protection you will need."

As soon as the soft linen fell across
his body, Tom felt a wave of warmth
drive the chill from his bones.

Elenna closed her eyes and stroked
the cloak. "It's like the cosiest fleece
I've ever worn!" she said.

Tom stroked the thin material in
amazement as Rana grinned at him.
"Thank you!" he said. "It must have
been strong magic that spun this!"

"Magic?" The tallest man chuckled
– though Tom thought he sounded a
little nervous. "There's no magic here!"

"The fabric is from our own looms,"
said Rana, "and the linen comes
from a special flax that only grows
in our valley. We've learned over the
centuries how to weave clothes that

are light, but warm." She laughed, and
her companions joined in. "We've no
need for magic."

"Whatever it is, thank you for your
kindness!" Elenna said, rubbing her
cheek against her cloak.

Tom stroked the linen with
his fingers, shaking his head in
amazement. "No deerskin ever felt so
warm. You've saved our lives!"

CHAPTER THREE

THE BEAST OF THE MOUNTAINS

Tom's cloak flapped in the breeze as he surveyed the frozen landscape. The sun was rising higher now, dazzling them. Ahead, the snow-covered wastes and jagged hills stretched to the distant horizon. It was a desert of snow and ice, and there was no sign of the glowing red cobblestones that marked the Warrior's Road.

Reaching into the folds of his cloak, Tom drew out the map. He frowned, inspecting the lines and contours. *We've been saved from freezing – but we're no further forward on our Quest.*

Elenna studied the map over his shoulder, then gazed over the horizon. "The snow's hidden all the landmarks."

Tom shivered – not from the cold this time. *In this desolate place, the Judge doesn't have to set us traps. We could be defeated just by the weather!*

"Don't worry, Tom," Elenna murmured, as if reading his thoughts. "We'll find the way forward. You've been Master of the Beasts, remember?"

"And I will be again," agreed Tom.

But for the first time, he found himself wondering if they really could conquer the challenges of the Warrior's Road. *I'm beginning to see why so many before me failed this task...*

"We have to get down from here, surely?" Elenna said. "All we need is a route out of the mountains."

Tom turned to their new friends. "Could you show us the way down?"

"We can do better than that," said the tall bearded man. "We'll take you with us part of the way."

Tom was surprised by the man's offer. "But why—"

He smiled. "It's on our way, and besides – you have a sword. If we meet a fierce animal..."

"I'll willingly protect you," said Tom.

Rana nodded. "Then it's agreed!" she said. "We can lead you safely on a path out of here."

As they set off through the snowy

land, cloaks flapping around their
shoulders, Tom noticed the young girl
Maya drop back to walk beside Silver
and Elenna. She ruffled Silver's fur as
she walked, crooning to him happily.

"Maya seems to like Silver," Tom
told Rana as she strode at his side.

"I'm glad she isn't afraid of him,"
she agreed. "There are so many tales
of the Fox-Beast in these mountains,

I thought she might be too nervous to approach your wolf."

"Silver isn't dangerous," Tom assured her. "He would never hurt Maya. But could you tell me about this Fox-Beast?" He didn't want to panic Rana, but he needed to find out if this creature was the one he needed to defeat.

Rana's expression darkened. "We call the creature Targro. He takes the form of a fox – but he's huge, and utterly terrifying. It's said he has a coat of fire, and vicious spikes that run along his back. He hides himself beneath the snow, ambushing any traveller unlucky enough to stumble upon him."

"So that's why you were alarmed when you found us hiding in the snow!" said Tom.

"We couldn't be sure." Rana shook her head. "None of us have seen the creature. Our route has always taken us across the mountains, and that's a risk we must take. But why are you and your friend here? You still haven't told us."

Tom thought quickly. "Elenna and I live in a valley nearby," he said, hoping his lies wouldn't be too obvious. He didn't want to make up stories, but it was best these people didn't know about the Beasts. "We brought Silver into the hills for a hunt. He needs a good run now and again. But we got...lost."

Quickening his pace, Tom drew a little ahead. He didn't feel the cold at all now, thanks to his cloak. For an instant the sun blazed directly into his eyes. It was hard to make out the path, though he could feel the ground beginning to slope down beneath his feet. But suddenly it grew steeper. Then the soles of his boots began to slide, and Tom gave a cry as he stumbled to a halt. When he held a hand to his eyes, finally he could see what lay before him.

The snow-covered track had vanished into thin air, leaving behind nothing but a deadly fall towards the valley below.

If I had taken just one more step, he thought, *I would be dead now.*

CHAPTER FOUR

A DANGEROUS CHOICE

A gust of wind snatched Tom's cloak
and whirled it around him. One of
the men behind cried out a warning,
and Maya gave a small scream. Rana
snatched Tom's arm and drew him
back. "Careful! Didn't you see the
drop?"

"The sun blinded me." His heart
thudding, Tom stumbled back and

45

leaned against the solid rock face,
noticing that the others had halted
safely before the precipice. *I shouldn't
have charged ahead*, he thought, angry
with himself. *I have to remember that
I don't know this land!*

Elenna laid a hand on his arm. "Be

careful, Tom," she said. "That was too close!"

"I know," he muttered. Once again Tom shoved his flapping cloak aside, hands shaking. Taking deep breaths, he unfurled the map. All he could do was pick out landmarks and contours as best he could by their snow-covered shapes around him. "But we have to keep going this way. Look!"

Elenna traced a line on the map with her finger. "This shows the Warrior's Road going straight ahead – into that valley." She raised her head to gaze at the lip of the terrifying cliff.

"Then that's where we must go," Tom said grimly. "One way or another, we'll have to get down that precipice."

"It won't be easy." Elenna approached the edge, eyeing the

drop. Silver paced anxiously at her side, hackles bristling.

Rana looked from Tom to Elenna, and gave a short, disbelieving laugh. "You plan to go that way? Down the cliff?"

Tom nodded. "We don't have a choice. That's where the map is telling us to go."

Rana looked puzzled, but then she shrugged. "You must really trust that map. Well, that's your choice. I'll ask no more questions. We'll leave you now. We go this way." Rana pointed to another path – a twisting narrow passage in the rocks behind them.

Gazing along it, Tom could see a cleft in the mountains beyond, and a distant smudge of ice-covered sea. For a moment, he felt tempted to stay with their new companions, to take the easier road in the company of friendly strangers – but he shook his head.

"We're grateful for your help," Tom told her.

Rana sighed. "I have no idea what strange mission you are on, but I wish you luck with it."

"And stay away from Fox-Beasts!" warned Maya. The little girl gave Silver a final hug.

"Oh!" Tom remembered suddenly. "We must return your cloaks!" He began to slip the fabric from his shoulders, and instantly felt the sharp bite of the wind on his skin.

"No!" Rana raised a hand, shaking her head. "Keep the cloaks, with our blessing. Out here, your lives may depend on them."

Tom was glad to pull the warm

cloak round his shoulders once more. "Thank you."

"You're very kind," said Elenna, snuggling into her own cloak. "A safe journey to all of you!"

Tom and Elenna waved their goodbyes and watched as their friends set off into the narrow cleft in the rocks, their loose, light clothing fluttering in the cold breeze. Beside Elenna, Silver gave a soft mournful whine.

"You liked Maya, didn't you?" Elenna laughed, ruffling the wolf's fur. "If you're not careful, I'll be jealous!"

Silver nuzzled her hand, then glanced back at the sheer cliff.

Tom frowned. Down the cliff face he could make out faint traces of red cobbles, in tiny patches where the snow had slipped and broken away. The Warrior's Road definitely led that way. It seemed such a faint and hopeless path to follow, so full of dangers. *Almost impossible...* Tom shivered. As he pulled his cloak tighter around his body for comfort, all that gripped him was a feeling of loneliness and despair.

What's the matter with me? Tom shook himself, angry. It wasn't like him to feel so defeated!

"Can you see anything?" Elenna interrupted his dark thoughts. "Is there any sign of the Warrior's Road?"

"Not much – a path," he told her, "but it's very narrow."

Just looking at the cliff made Tom's head sway. *Elenna's always hated heights*, he thought. *Maybe I should tell her to go with the others.*

To his relief, though, his friend was already on her knees at the edge of the cliff, testing the firmness of the ground, prodding it with her fingers. Just below her, a stunted plant grew in a small crack. Elenna grasped it and tugged it free with ease, then held it out to Tom.

"Better not rely on these to support us!" she told him.

Tom nodded, admiring his friend's bravery. He expected a rush of determination to flood through him, but he felt... *Nothing*, he thought. *I don't feel scared, or courageous, or anything.* It was as if he suddenly didn't care about his Quest any more, or the Warrior's Road – or even about defeating the Judge. Tom slapped his hand against his head, hoping he could bang some sense into himself.

But even that didn't help. And his
fingers were cold. He curled them
into the cloak, and drew it tighter
around his body.

Silver tilted his head at Tom and
gave a questioning whine.

Tom gritted his teeth. "While there's
blood in my veins, I'll see this Quest
through!" he cried. But for the first
time in his life, the words felt empty
and meaningless...

CHAPTER FIVE

TERROR ON THE PRECIPICE

He kneeled down at Elenna's side, studying the sheer wall of rock. What else could he do? He had to go on. The sun shone fiercely in the cold sky, making the smooth granite gleam with a blinding dazzle. Tom rubbed his eyes, then sat back on his haunches so that he could rest his eyes from the glare. It was as if the cliff was carved out of brilliantly polished marble.

"How do we get down that?" he muttered. Tom couldn't even call on the powers of his shield, because the Judge had stripped him of its tokens' magic.

Elenna's eyes brightened as she leaped to her feet. "Remember Skurik?"

"Oh, yes," exclaimed Tom. "The Forest Demon left us gloves once we had defeated him."

He rummaged in his tunic, and pulled them out. The gloves looked fragile, like shrivelled, dried-up tree gum, but when Tom pulled them on, he felt the strength and power that they carried. Something told him they would prove vital on this latest Quest.

"If those are as sticky as the ooze that Skurik used to trap the children,

56

they'll really help," said Elenna.

Tom kneeled once more at the edge
of the precipice, and leaned down to
touch the rock wall. Sure enough, his
gloved hands clung firmly to the sheer
cliff-face.

"Perfect!" exclaimed Elenna, a gleam
in her eye. "That means you'll be able

to climb down – but what about Silver and me?"

For a strange and dizzying moment, a horrible thought went through Tom's mind: *That's your problem, not mine.*

Shocked at himself, he shook his head. *What made me think that?*

Still, he felt impatient as he peered around the cliff and down towards the valley. "Look, the Warrior's Road makes a bit of a path – can you see the line of it there? You know how sure-footed Silver is – he can make his way down almost by instinct. There's no other way, unless we leave him here."

Doubtfully, Elenna studied the faint scratch that was all they could see of the path. "Silver might manage that mountain track, but I won't," she said. "Look how it crumbles at the edges."

Tom examined the gloves, clenching and unclenching his fists and feeling the stickiness of the strange substance. "I think these would support the weight of both of us. I can carry you."

"Let's hope so," laughed Elenna, a little nervously as she clambered up onto a low outcrop of rock, then gripped Tom's back tightly. Tom waited while she used a strip of leather from her quiver to strap the two of them together.

"Ready," she said at last, tightening the last knot. Her voice trembled just a little.

Trying not to think about the endless drop below them, Tom lowered himself carefully over the cliff. He held his breath, not wanting to let go of the edge.

No. We must do this now, or never!

Easing one hand free, he lowered himself, then found another handhold below it. *And now there's no going back...*

Sure enough, the gloves stuck almost too tightly to the smooth rock. The strange substance stretched like rubber, clinging to every handhold, and Tom's muscles soon ached from tugging his hands loose. Each time he did, the gloves snapped back into shape with a sharp whack that made him wince.

And it didn't help that Elenna's grip felt like a stranglehold, or that her breathing was rapid and heavy on his neck.

"Elenna, are you all right?" he panted.

"I'm fine." His friend's voice was tight and high-pitched. Against his

back Tom could feel her thudding
heartbeat through his thin cloak.

"Not much further," he gasped,
risking a glance down. *That isn't quite
true*, he thought to himself, as fear

quickened his breathing.

A pale shadow flickered at the edge of his vision. It was probably just Silver, picking his way down the treacherous path, but Tom didn't dare turn his head to look properly. Yet again he tore his hand free of the cliff, and found another small spur of rock to cling to. His muscles were burning with pain, but the ground still seemed so terribly far away. Tom closed his eyes briefly, pressing his forehead to the icy rock as he caught his breath and steadied himself.

One handhold at a time, Tom. One handhold at a time...

A dizzying tide of relief swept through him. The ground was no more than a few arms' lengths below them!

As his feet found solid earth, Tom

was shaking. His legs felt weak with the effort of the climb.

"We've made it!" he said.

CHAPTER SIX

THE FIELD OF BONES

Loosening her grip at last, Elenna blew out a shaky breath. With trembling fingers she unfastened the leather strap that tied them together.

Her face grew serious as she gazed around at the valley. "Not everyone was as lucky as we were."

Cruel rocks jutted from the barren ground, and boulders were scattered

through tough grass that was crusted
with ice and patches of snow. Tom
rubbed sweat from his eyes. His heart
lurched when he realised what he
was looking at.

"They're not just rocks and
boulders," he breathed. "They're...
bones. Human bones!"

They lay scattered at the foot of the cliff. Tattered bits of clothing had caught on stunted thorn-bushes, and various bones were scattered beside one particularly vicious jagged rock. Close to a skeleton hand was a long dagger with a rust-tinged handle.

Elenna crouched to pick up the dagger. She stood up and tucked it into her belt. "Any weapon can be useful on a Beast Quest."

Tom stepped carefully through the field of bones. A clear track wound into the distance, a shimmering red ribbon of cobbles edged with snow.

"Look, Elenna." He pointed. "The Warrior's Road!"

"I can't see it, remember!" Elenna said, rolling her eyes. "But if you say it's there, I'll walk with you."

Behind them, there was a sharp

howl as Silver leaped down the last outcrop of rock and raced to join them, his tail lashing.

"Silver!" cried Elenna, rubbing his mane. "You made it!"

Tom huddled into his cloak as he listlessly watched his two friends greet each other. *Why don't I feel more glad that Silver's made it down safely?* None of it seemed important. Now that they were safely back on the ground, he couldn't even find it in him to think much about the Quest.

He shrugged. "We should go on. At least the Road is free of snow."

Not a speck of ice was visible on the red surface, which gleamed in the winter sun. Perhaps the Road was warm enough to melt any snow that touched it? Stepping onto it and removing the gloves, Tom crouched to touch the cobbles.

He snatched his hand back. No – the surface was icy cold. *It must be magic*, Tom thought. *Evil magic?* But whatever it was, Tom knew they had to follow the red cobblestones.

Before they could take a step, Silver gave a sudden sharp yelp of warning. Tail stiff, hackles bristling, he snarled at the sky.

"Silver's seen something," Elenna said, pointing upwards.

Squinting into the bright winter sky, Tom spotted the silhouette of a huge bird. It flapped awkwardly, and its high-pitched cries seemed distressed.

"It's a snow-owl," said Elenna, as the creature swooped lower. Now Tom could see its beautiful white plumage – and the spatters of blood that marked its wings. He frowned as the owl's flight dipped. Something seemed wrong.

"It's gone down into that valley. No – there it is again!" Elenna shielded her eyes against the glare. "And it's coming closer!"

Tom spotted something dangling from its clawed feet. Soon he could make out that it was a tethering rope, swinging wildly beneath the bird.

"It's a hunting owl," he said. "It

belongs to someone."

"It looks like it's trying to get our attention," said Elenna. "Maybe its owner is hurt."

"The *owl* is definitely hurt, Elenna," said Tom, clenching his fists. "Look at the blood on its wings. Something bad has happened here! We need to find out."

Never on his Quests had Tom turned away from an animal or person in need.

And if there is one thing we've learned, Tom thought, *it's that where there's blood, there's usually a Beast...*

CHAPTER SEVEN

THE BITE OF THE BEAST

Tom sprang down from the cobbled track and ran towards the hidden valley. Above him the blood-spattered owl circled, screeching. It seemed to be leading him towards a dark cleft in the hills.

"Tom, wait!" shouted Elenna.

He stopped and turned, irritated. "What is it?" he called.

"Don't be in such a rush." His friend caught up, Silver panting at her side. "Should we really abandon the Warrior's Road? The Judge has set you a Quest, remember?"

"But someone's in trouble!" he said.

"We don't know that for sure," Elenna pointed out. "It could be a trick to lure you."

Tom sighed. "Even if it is," he said, "I can't just walk away from someone in trouble."

Elenna nodded slowly. "Just be careful," she warned. "Don't risk the whole Quest!"

Resentment prickled Tom's spine as he drew his cloak closer around him. *Does she always have to be so bossy?*

"What's the point of the Quest, anyway?" he snapped. "The Judge will do as he likes! He always does!"

Instantly, he felt guilt squirm in his stomach as Elenna's mouth fell open with shock.

"I've never heard you talk like that," she said. She reached out a hand to Tom, but he pulled away.

What am I thinking? he wondered, horrified at the words that had come out of his mouth. Yet he couldn't stop thinking of all the Quests he had completed and the dangers he had faced – and the Judge had just snatched his triumphs away so easily. Was it really worth risking his life facing the challenge of the Warrior's Road?

Elenna doesn't understand!

He turned sharply away from his friend, unwilling to meet her eyes. His cloak, caught by a gust of wind, wound so tightly around his body that he had to fight to free his arm and clutch the hilt of his sword.

Tom tugged his blade awkwardly from its scabbard and strode on. The snow-owl still circled in the air above them. Glancing back, he saw that

Elenna was following him, a little warily – but he was pleased to see her own cloak was wrapped tightly around her. The chill wind was rising again and they both needed to stay warm.

"Tom!" gasped Elenna, pointing ahead. "You were right. There is someone there – someone injured!"

Tom took a breath as he squinted into the distance. A man was slumped against an icy boulder. The owl swooped down and landed on the man's shoulder, then swivelled its head and glared at Tom with its huge orange eyes.

Tom plunged forward. The snow seemed to grow deeper with every step, and his legs ached with the effort – yet he struggled on, moving further and further away from the

Warrior's Road. Glancing back once, he saw how small it looked now. How unimportant...

Would it really matter if I couldn't find it again?

Tom kneeled at the wounded man's side. His ice-frosted eyelids were closed and he was pale as death.

A low groan of pain came from his cracked mouth as a pool of blood soaked his tunic front. His face and hands were scratched and injured.

"What happened to you?" asked Tom.

Slowly the man's eyes opened, and he blinked away dried blood. There was terror in his gaze as he snatched feebly at Tom's cloak.

"My name...is Luke. Moray and I..." His voice was hoarse and Tom had to lean closer to hear his words. "...were attacked...out of nowhere. By some kind of...savage monster!"

Tom's heart pounded. "What kind of monster?"

"Like a fox," the man said, wheezing. "But a bigger fox than you could ever imagine!"

Targro... thought Tom, remembering

the name the snow-walkers had given the Beast. He squeezed Luke's shoulder gently, feeling a brief surge of anger in his heart. Why would a guardian of the Road attack an innocent man? Was Targro an Evil Beast? Whatever it took, he had to rid this land of such a terror!

Yet, almost immediately, his heart sank. *But there will only be more Beasts, bigger and stronger – more deadly. I can never defeat them all...*

Elenna was at his side, pulling her bag of herbs from her pack. "Try not to move," she told Luke. "I can help you. And Moray too."

Yes, if Elenna can help this man, she will – and so should I! Tom told himself. *How could I ever have thought anything else?*

"Tell me more about the Beast," he

urged the injured hunter.

Luke gave a gasp of pain as Elenna pressed a poultice of herbs and melted snow against a horrible slash on his shoulder. "Deadly spines on its back. Huge claws – and the teeth! Savage, ripping teeth—"

Elenna glanced at Tom, looking worried. Whatever she did, Luke's wounds would not stop leaking blood-drops onto the snow. She reached out a hand to the snow-owl, trying to clean its wings, but it flinched away with an angry screech of fright.

"We've got to do something," whispered Elenna to Tom. "But what? I don't know if I can help either of them." She got to her feet, and Tom too began to stand up.

A grip like a vice clutched Tom's leg.

He stared down and saw that Luke was clinging to him with bloodied fingers.

"No! You can't go now!" he cried. There was an evil light in Luke's eyes, and his voice was a vicious hiss. Above him, flapping wildly again, the snow-owl gave an eerie screech of horror.

"Let go!" Tom said, trying to pull himself free.

But Luke jerked him forward again, and Tom staggered to keep his footing.

"Stay here, you fool," the man

snarled. "And face your death!"

Luke bared his teeth in a horrible grin of triumph. He threw back his head and laughed – a screech like an owl's cry.

"Tom!" shouted Elenna.

But Tom had already caught the awful stench. It was like the breath of a giant monster, hot against his neck. Luke's laughter became high and hysterical as a shadow fell across them both.

Tom knew in his heart that it was the shadow of a Beast.

"Die, boy!" Luke cried with twisted delight. His glance shifted to whatever it was that stood over Tom. "Die at the claws of Targro!"

CHAPTER EIGHT

THE ARCTIC MENACE STRIKES

Wrenching himself free of Luke's grip, Tom whirled round. Above him towered a colossal creature. It cast such a dark shadow that all Tom could make out were two huge eyes, glittering with hatred and fixed directly on him.

Targro's purple fur glowed in the cold sunlight, but glinting even

brighter were his long cruel claws,
like great shards of ice. Vicious spines
ran the length of his back and tail.
The Beast's pointed snout gleamed

with huge, wicked teeth, flecked
with drool – and the blood of his last
victim.

Targro gave a high shriek of rage,
spraying saliva that splashed Tom's
face. Rearing up, a massive black
shape against the sun, Targro raised
his murderous ice-claws, then
brought them slashing down towards
Elenna.

Silver bounded aside as Tom sprang
towards his friend, pushing her
clear of Targro's lethal strike. Tom's
momentum sent him slamming into
a rock. He felt the rush of air past his
ear as a massive paw hit the ground
beside him.

Roaring, the Beast turned its fury
on the wounded hunter who lay
helpless against the cliff. Targro sank
his claws into the man's chest, lifted

him and hurled him aside. "No!" Tom
tried to shout, but no sound came
from his winded lungs as Luke's body
smashed into a rock. Up in the sky,
the snow-owl Moray gave a scream of
distress and pain.

Clutching Silver's fur as he snarled
at Targro, Elenna stumbled up out of
the snow and reached for her bow,
loosing arrow after arrow at the
Beast. One of them found its mark,
striking deep into Targro's shoulder
fur.

For a moment Tom thought the
Beast would lunge for Elenna. But
as Targro reared up, Moray swooped
straight across his sightline, before
shooting towards a high outcrop of
rock.

Roaring at the owl, Targro spun on
his hind legs and gave chase.

Staggering upright at last, Tom felt a surge of rage. Luke was left here wounded…as bait! This had all been a trick to lure him away from the Warrior's Road.

Sickness churned in Tom's belly. This Quest was beginning to feel hopeless.

Why try? he thought. *I can't fight this kind of evil!*

Tom seized the hilt of his sword, dragging it from its scabbard. *No…I can still fight! But the sword feels so heavy.* Tom wrested the blade from its scabbard. As he struggled to lift his weapon, strength seemed to leak from his muscles, taking all his fury with it. He let his arm drop back to his side.

His cloak twisted snugly around him, making every movement slow and awkward.

"Tom!" cried Elenna. "Your sword!"

The weapon had fallen from his hand. It lay there, glinting with an icy light. There seemed barely any point in reaching for it, but Elenna dived towards the hilt. Snatching it up, she held it out for him.

"Tom – what's wrong?" she asked, worry creasing her brow.

What was wrong? His fingers curled round the hilt – his own trusty blade, but it still felt strangely heavy. His cloak flapped and tightened around his body, even though the wind had died down. Tom tried to loosen it, but it clung even tighter.

Too tight! he realised with a bolt of fear.

Now Elenna was also tearing at her cloak. Her mouth opened, as if she was trying to gasp words, but all she could manage was a strangled splutter. Silver was howling in fear, but there was nothing the wolf could do.

"There's something wrong with the cloaks!" Tom cried. "Something evil." Why had it taken him so long to understand?

Elenna sank to her knees in the snow, her skin flushing deep red as she struggled to breathe. Tom wanted to help, but he too was sucking desperately for tiny gulps of air. Pain stabbed his lungs, as if iron bands were tightening around his chest with every moment.

Freeing one hand, Elenna made a desperate grab at her quiver, and seized the dagger they had found beneath the cliff. With fire in her eyes, she slashed the dagger down, cutting the throttling cloak. With a loud ripping sound, the garment fell from her shoulders.

She leaped to her feet, gasping and wheezing. "Tom! Free yourself!"

But as Tom wrestled with his cloak, he could see Elenna's teeth were chattering, and she shivered and shook from the bitterly cold air. Tom saw the whole cunning wickedness of the plan now. *If we don't wear the cloaks, we'll freeze to death – but if we keep them on, they might suffocate us.*

"It must have been those travellers," Elenna said. She was trying to help Tom tear the cloak from his shoulders, but it was too dangerous for her to use the dagger on him, too. One wrong move, and she'd stab him. "Those travellers must have been in the pay of the Judge all along."

Why couldn't he get free? With every wriggle and push, the cloak seemed to tighten around him even more. It had a life of its own! He could feel his ribs creaking from the pressure and his fingertips were turning white.

Then Tom heard a thundering of

paws, a grunting of furious breath, a low ominous growling. Turning rapidly, he almost slipped and fell as the ground shook beneath his feet. Though his vision was blurred, he saw cold sunlight glowing on purple fur, vicious spines and slavering jaws.

Targro!

The Beast was back, pounding through the snow and swinging his tail like a lethal club. Elenna grabbed Tom and shoved him aside. Silver snarled and snapped, scampering away from Targro's tail and claws. The wolf tumbled over and over, sending snow flying.

I have to free myself to fight this Beast, Tom realised, as his cloak continued to tighten around him. *Or I'll die – and the Judge will have total control of Avantia!*

CHAPTER NINE

A DEADLY DUEL

Tom fell to his knees, desperate for breath. His vision was darkening, and he was only just able to see Elenna's grim face as she ripped at his cloak.

"Targro's attacking again!" she cried. "Come on, Tom – breathe!"

Tom could not reply. Silver was snarling at the Beast, holding him at bay for now, but soon Targro might kill the wolf with a single swipe of his paws.

"The cloaks – they drained our strength! Those snow-walkers betrayed us." In desperation, Elenna pulled out her dagger. She cut and slashed until only shreds of the cloak hung from Tom's neck and shoulders. He could feel the trickle of blood down his chest, but he was fairly sure there'd been no serious injury.

Almost instantly, the bite of cold air pinched at his limbs. Urgency flooded his body. He was no longer under the magic spell. It was time to battle this Beast!

Targro's spiked tail swung at him as Tom's enemy let out a huge roar. Tom leaped out of the way just in time, his strength returning. The tail slammed into a boulder, sending out sparks.

Silver sprang forward, but the Beast
was many times his size – and with
a much longer reach. Tom couldn't
risk lashing out with his sword while
the wolf darted between him and his
opponent.

"Elenna, call Silver!" he shouted.

As Elenna dragged her snarling wolf

away, Tom dived between Targro's giant paws, sending snow flying. To be able to strike at the Beast's body he would have to climb onto it. He reached out, but as soon as his hands came in contact with Targro's pelt, he could feel the freezing slipperiness of his stinking coat. There was no way Tom could climb up there without help.

The gloves! he thought. *The gloves I won from Skurik!*

As the Beast tried to claw at Tom beneath his belly, Tom pulled the slimy gloves onto his hands. He gripped a purple-furred foreleg and swiftly climbed up, hand over hand, until he was beyond the reach of those deadly claws. He gained precious seconds while the Beast flailed, confused – but soon Targro felt

Tom's weight. He lunged viciously and snapped his teeth, but Tom was nearly at the Beast's shoulder now. With a final heave, he pulled himself up, reaching for the spines on Targro's back.

The Beast whipped his body from side to side, snarling with frustration – but with Skurik's slime-gloves, Tom's grip was firm. Clutching fistfuls of fur, he hauled himself up to Targro's neck and clung there.

The Fox-Beast roared, shaking his body violently from head to tail, then launched himself forward, thundering through the snow as Tom held on for dear life.

There was a strange, smudged line at the edge of Tom's vision. Too late, he recognised a gleam of light on crusted ice ahead. Then he noticed blue sky, and the powdery cloud of snow blown by wind into thin air. He and Targro were heading straight for the edge of a great bank of ice and rock!

"Back!" yelled Tom, hauling uselessly on Targro's fur. But the Beast beneath him slithered and toppled, and they plunged down the cliff together.

Tom sucked in an icy breath of terror. For a moment he felt weightless, plummeting through empty sky.

Then something snatched him from the air with a jolt, and the breath was knocked from his body. His head whirled. *What—*

One of the ragged tatters of his cloak had caught on a stunted tree, leaving him dangling as Targro crashed to the ground far below. Tom saw snow explode, and the Beast was enveloped in a cloud of white.

The last shreds of Tom's cloak blustered in his face. *I'm still not out of danger*, he thought. *I have to get rid of this evil thing!*

Gritting his teeth, Tom hacked the point of his sword into the cloak, and sawed determinedly back and forth.

The fabric tore with a sound like a shriek. Freed from the cloak, Tom slid loose – and felt himself begin to plummet. He snatched for the tree...

...but his fingers missed.

I'm going to die!

Tom landed hard, feeling as if his limbs and all his teeth had been shaken loose. The impact punched the air from his lungs and his head spun so violently that it took a long moment before he realised that he was still alive – half buried in a deep drift of snow.

Aching, trembling, he struggled to all fours. Now he felt his anger and his energy return.

"Face me, Targro!" Tom stood and gripped his sword two-handed.

But the Fox-Beast was nowhere in sight. Cold air hit Tom with its full force, chilling him to the bone. He'd rid himself of the evil magic of the cloak, but now he had no guard against the weather. He and Elenna could die out here!

"Elenna," he shouted up. Her worried face appeared at the edge. "Throw me your dagger!"

"Here!" Flashing in the light, the blade spun through the air. Tom had to dodge its lethal tip as it smacked into the snow.

He had two weapons now. *Let Targro try his best!*

A blade in each hand, Tom turned a full circle, searching for his adversary. He stood in a shallow valley, enclosed by cliffs against which snow was piled, half concealing deep caves. Could Targro be hiding in one of them? Surely an Evil Beast would not give up so easily?

Something's wrong...

A shiver of alarm went down Tom's spine – and in that instant, the snow beside him erupted. Targro roared and struck out with his tail.

Tom threw himself aside, dodging the spikes and getting behind the

Beast. This was his chance!

His resin gloves still on his hands, Tom flung himself up onto the Beast's tail, and held tight.

Targro howled, lashing his tail violently, but Tom clung on, and began to climb. One spine after another, he hauled himself up and further up. *I have to get to his back, where he can't reach me*, Tom told himself. He was so close. Only a few more spines...

At last he was on Targro's back, wriggling forward between the longest spikes. The Fox-Beast writhed in fury, roaring as he tossed his head and kicked with his hind legs, trying to throw off his attacker. Tom now had respite from the thrashing of the tail, but Targro's struggles were throwing up plumes of stinging snow, and Tom had to shut his eyes tight to protect them. Lunging forwards, he dragged himself up the Beast's neck and onto his head.

He can't bite me here, thought Tom grimly, *though he might shake me to death!*

Almost blinded, Tom fumbled a hand down between the Beast's eyes. Seizing the Beast's snout, he gripped it with his gloved fingers.

Targro's angry cries rose to a frenzied shriek. But with his firm grip on the Beast's flesh, Tom managed to twist his huge head round. Targro's jaws snapped wildly, but Tom was out of his reach – and the Beast couldn't see where he was going.

Out of the corner of his eye, Tom saw Elenna scrambling down the cliff. Gripping her bow, she was running to find a good shot at the Beast.

Tom took a breath to shout a warning – Elenna was running below a crust of snow that had built up perilously at the top of the cliff. But suddenly, as Elenna sprinted clear of the shadow of the cornice, Tom saw his chance to end this battle once and for all.

Directly beneath that fragile crust of snow was the darkness of a cave. *And that's where Targro's heading now!*

"Elenna!" yelled Tom. "The cave! Ahead of you!" He risked loosening a hand to make a rolling signal. "Send the snow down!"

Elenna nodded and raced back up towards the cliff-top. Above the cave and the cornice of snow, she climbed higher up the sloping ground.

Tom clung on as Targro bounded

towards the rockface, howling and snarling and thrashing. Through half-blinded eyes, Tom could see Elenna already sending a ball of snow rolling down the slope. It grew as it picked up speed...

Beneath Tom, Targro plunged on, careering towards the cave-mouth.

I have to time this exactly right!

Elenna's now enormous snowball had built up its own momentum. As it slammed into the massive crust of snow, Tom heard a crack like thunder. The whole cornice trembled, then shattered and collapsed. Letting go of Targro's snout, Tom flung himself off his back as the Beast careered madly on towards the cave.

The avalanche crashed down in an explosion of white. Rolling clear, Tom heard the Beast's furious shrieks as

the gigantic slabs of snow fell. Targro's cries grew muffled, and the snow began to settle as the last chunks of the cornice tumbled down. By the time Tom could clamber to his feet, there was no sound or movement.

The Beast was entombed in snow.

CHAPTER TEN

RETURN TO THE WARRIOR'S ROAD

The world seemed suddenly very silent. Nothing stirred beneath the vast heap of snow where Targro lay. Panting, Tom glanced up to see Elenna scrambling down the hill towards him, Silver at her heels.

Tom's eye was caught by a bright gleam on the ice. He crouched to pick up the object.

"What's that?" asked Elenna.

"It's another token," said Tom, turning it in his hands. "From Targro."

It was a single claw from the Fox-Beast. Razor-sharp edges glittered in the sun like diamonds, and Tom knew that the claw would make a fine throwing weapon. He tucked it carefully into his belt.

"We did it, Elenna!" His grin faded as he remembered the murdered hunter. "Except...we did not save Luke."

"Targro is to blame for that," said Elenna firmly. "You avenged Luke."

Yes, thought Tom. *And his death makes me all the more determined to see this Quest through, and become Master of the Beasts once again...*

"Come on," Elenna said. Her breath was like smoke on the freezing air. "We have to get out of this cold. It wouldn't be very good to defeat Targro, only to freeze to death ourselves!"

Tom tugged out his map and pointed at a thin line of red that cut across the contours. "We've wandered far off course – which I'm sure was the Judge's plan all along. But look –

is this a shortcut back?"

"The line's very faint," said Elenna doubtfully.

"Yes – but look ahead there," Tom argued, "where the snow's shallower. I'm sure that's the line on the map. It has to be worth a try!"

The snow wasn't as deep on the path, but their leggings still became soaked and freezing within a few steps. Still Tom ploughed on, muscles aching, fighting the desire to stop and rest.

Elenna was shivering violently. Tom's throat felt cracked with cold. Even Silver struggled, with his fur crusted with ice. As the three of them reached the top of a low rise, Tom gave a hoarse cry of recognition.

"The Warrior's Road!" he gasped.

They stumbled down the

last bank onto the glowing red cobbles. Elenna's teeth chattered uncontrollably, and Silver nudged closely against her as they trudged on.

"Tom," Elenna rasped. "Is that... smoke?"

Tom squinted ahead. There was a silver line between two hills; something like mist hung above it. "I think it's...steam! There must be water – warm water!"

As they stumbled forward down the slope of the Road, Silver bounded down a snowy bank and leaped into the water with a huge splash. Laughing breathlessly with relief, Tom and Elenna plunged in after him.

It was a volcanic lake, Tom realised – blissfully hot, instantly thawing their aching and frozen bodies. Tom grinned at Elenna as she submerged

herself up to her chin, her eyes twinkling with pleasure. He sighed and lay back too, enjoying the warmth.

For an age they wallowed, reluctant to emerge once more into the icy world.

"This lake has saved our lives," said Elenna, smiling. "But I suppose we'll have to get out eventually!"

Pushing his wet hair out of his eyes, Tom swam to the edge and hauled himself out of the water, expecting a chill blast of wind.

But none came. In fact, the air seemed surprisingly warm. The snow sparkled extra bright, and even as Tom watched, it seemed to turn as fragile as crystal. Great swathes of it were melting, letting bits of grass and bracken poke through the thawing crust. The green-and-brown patches grew swiftly bigger as runnels of meltwater formed into streams and trickled towards the steaming lake. A warm breeze caressed Tom's skin, and he could hear the distant drip of fast-melting ice.

Elenna waded out of the lake, and Silver shook water from his shaggy coat. All three of them turned, gazing at the greening landscape as the last of the snow vanished.

Elenna scowled. "You'd almost think someone had magicked the mountains to be cold – just for us."

Tom nodded, feeling a swell of anger in his chest. "I'm sure someone did. And I'm just as sure that it was the Judge!"

Elenna raised an eyebrow at him. "What about Maya and her mother?" she said. "They gave us those treacherous cloaks. They must have been working for him, too."

Tom nodded. "We've learned one lesson," he told his friend. "We need to be very careful about trusting the people we meet on this Beast Quest."

As they set out along the Warrior's Road once more, the sun was warm on Tom's skin. He tilted his face up to the soft blue sky. His eyes widened as he caught sight of a black speck, soaring far above them.

"Moray," Elenna said, pointing. "At least the owl survived."

"But we couldn't even trust a wild animal," said Tom. "Hopefully he's good again now that Targro has been defeated." The snow-owl gave a squawk as if telling Tom he was sorry for the trouble he'd caused.

Ahead of them, the Warrior's Road trailed towards the horizon, calling Tom forward to meet its next challenges. Four more Beasts awaited him…

…four more battles to test his claim to the title of Master of the Beasts.

Join Tom on the next stage
of the Beast Quest, when he faces

Slivka
the Cold-Hearted
Curse

Beast Quest ®

Series 13: THE WARRIOR'S ROAD
COLLECT THEM ALL!

The Warrior's Road is Tom's toughest challenge yet. Will he succeed where so many have failed?

978 1 40832 402 8

978 1 40832 403 5

978 1 40832 404 2

978 1 40832 405 9

978 1 40832 406 6

978 1 40832 407 3

Win an exclusive
Beast Quest T-shirt and goody bag!

In every Beast Quest book the Beast Quest logo is
hidden in one of the pictures. Find the logos in books
73 to 78 and make a note of which pages they appear
on. Write the six page numbers on a postcard and
send it in to us.
Each month we will draw one winner to receive
a Beast Quest T-shirt and goody bag.

THE BEAST QUEST COMPETITION:
The Warrior's Road
Orchard Books
338 Euston Road, London NW1 3BH
Australian readers should email:
childrens.books@hachette.com.au

New Zealand readers should write to:
Beast Quest Competition
4 Whetu Place, Mairangi Bay, Auckland, NZ
or email: childrensbooks@hachette.co.nz

Only one entry per child.
Final draw: January 2014

You can also enter this competition
via the Beast Quest website: www.beastquest.co.uk

Join the Quest,
Join the Tribe

www.beastquest.co.uk

Have you checked out the Beast Quest website?
It's the place to go for games, downloads, activities,
sneak previews and lots of fun!

You can read all about your favourite Beasts,
download free screensavers and desktop wallpapers
for your computer, and even challenge your friends
to a Beast Tournament.

Sign up to the newsletter at www.beastquest.co.uk
to receive exclusive extra content and the
opportunity to enter special members-only
competitions. We'll send you up-to-date info on all
the Beast Quest books, including the next exciting
series which features four brand-new Beasts!